MATTHEW AND THE

MIDNIGHT
HOSPITAL

Published in Canada in 1999 by
Stoddart Kids,
a division of Stoddart Publishing Co. Limited
34 Lesmill Road
Toronto, Canada M3B 2T6
Tel (416) 445-3333 Fax (416) 445-5967
E-mail Customer.Service@ccmailgw.genpub.com

Published in the United States in 1999 by
Stoddart Kids,
a division of Stoddart Publishing Co. Limited
180 Varick Street, 9th Floor
New York, New York 10014
Toll free 1-800-805-1083
E-mail gdsinc@genpub.com

Distributed in Canada by
General Distribution Services
325 Humber College Blvd.,
Toronto, ON M9W 7C3
Tel (416) 213-1919 Fax (416) 213-1917
E-mail Customer.Service@ccmailgw.genpub.com

Distributed in the United States by
General Distribution Services
85 River Rock Drive, Suite 202
Buffalo, New York 14207
Toll free 1-800-805-1083
E-mail gdsinc@genpub.com

Reprinted in September 1999

Canadian Cataloguing in Publication Data

Morgan, Allen, 1946–
Matthew and the midnight hospital

ISBN 0-7737-6014-8

I. Martchenko, Michael. II. Title.

PS8576.O642M3 1999   jC813'.54   C98-931791-9
PZ7.M66Ma 1999

*Matthew's dream takes him to the midnight hospital
where he is treated to a new Band-Aid and
some hilarious circus fun.*

THE CANADA COUNCIL | LE CONSEIL DES ARTS
FOR THE ARTS | DU CANADA
SINCE 1957 | DEPUIS 1957

*We acknowledge for their financial support of our publishing
program the Canada Council, the Ontario Arts Council, and
the Government of Canada through the Book Publishing
Industry Development Program (BPIDP).*

Printed and bound in Hong Kong, China by
Book Art Inc., Toronto

MATTHEW AND THE
MIDNIGHT
HOSPITAL

by Allen Morgan
Illustrated by Michael Martchenko

Stoddart
Kids
TORONTO • NEW YORK

One day when Matthew had nothing to do, he decided to start a circus. He was the clown and the ringmaster too.

"You can be my lion," he told his mother. "I'll make you a cage, and after I tame you, I'll teach you lots of amazing tricks."

His mother said she was busy right then, but she helped him with his costume, complete with bath towel cape.

"Let me know when it's time for the show," she said, as he went outside.

Matthew looked around for a few wild animals to train. The cat from next door wasn't all that keen, but a couple of squirrels up high in the tree were jumping from branch to branch.

"I'll do tricks down here while they do them up there," Matthew decided. He practiced a while and when he was ready, he shouted for his mom to come see the show.

"Ladies and gentlemen, boys and girls, here's Matthew the Magnificent and his amazing flying squirrels!" he announced.

Matthew went into his act. He balanced on chairs and jumped great gaps, he swung to new heights on his trapeze swing, and flew through the air right over the wading pool. All his tricks worked out quite well and his mother was very impressed. But just at the end, as he jumped onto the picnic table to take his bow, he tripped on his cape and fell.

"Whoa!" he yelled as he tumbled off. "Ow!" he yelped as he hit the ground. "Mom!" he cried when he saw his knee.

His mother brought out the first aid kit. She cleaned him up and put on a nice, new Band-Aid.

Matthew moaned. "I should probably go to Emergency."

His mother smiled. "Don't worry, dear. It's just a small scrape."

Matthew was sure it was much more than that, but before he could speak, one of the squirrels missed a branch overhead and fell to the ground at their feet. It lay there for a while without moving.

Matthew frowned. "Should we give him a Band-Aid too?" he asked.

"I'm afraid it wouldn't help," said his mother.

Matthew's mother wrapped the squirrel in an old kitchen towel and took it to the garage. As she tucked it into a small cardboard box, she shook her head.

"I'm afraid that's all we can do," she said.

"Is he dead?" Matthew asked.

"No he's not, but he is hurt. Just how badly I can't say. We'll have to wait till tomorrow to see if he'll be OK."

When Matthew got into bed that night, he was thinking about the squirrel.

"Will he get cold out in the garage?"

"I don't think so, dear," his mother replied. "He's wrapped up warm in his towel."

"I hope his family knows where he is," Matthew said.

"I'm sure they do. Don't lift your Band-Aid or it won't stay on."

"I just want to see if I'm getting better. If I get better, maybe the squirrel will too."

"He's gone to sleep now, and so should you," his mother said. Then she kissed him goodnight and turned off the light.

As Matthew lay awake all alone in the dark, he heard the wail of a siren somewhere far away. He curled himself up in his soft, warm blankets until he felt just like the squirrel. "Don't worry," he whispered. "We'll both get well." Then he closed his eyes. Soon he was fast asleep.

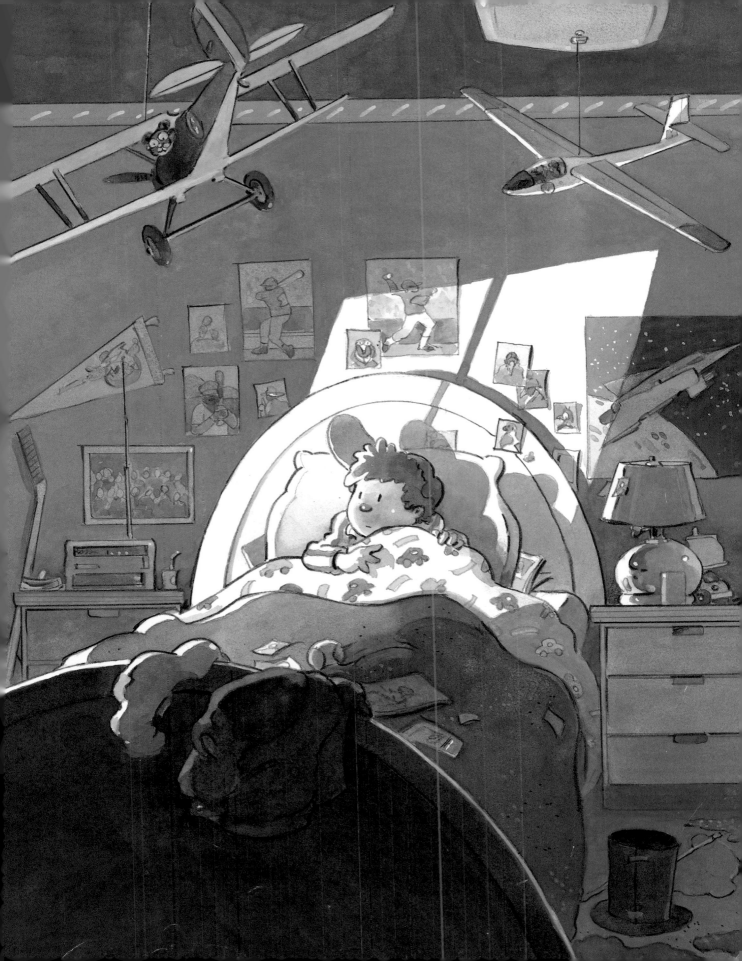

Around about midnight, Matthew woke up. A siren sounded loud and close by, so he got out of bed and went to the window. An ambulance was there.

Quick as a flash, Matthew dashed outside. As he arrived the ambulance guys were loading a stretcher into the back. The injured squirrel was strapped in tight.

"Will he be OK?" Matthew asked.

"Hard to say. Got to get to Emergency right away."

"I got hurt too," Matthew explained, and he pointed to his knee.

"Looks pretty bad," the man agreed. "You better come with us."

Matthew got in and hopped onto a stretcher. The driver slammed the door. A moment later, with the siren blaring, the ambulance pulled away.

When they arrived at the hospital, the waiting room was jammed. Still, the midnight nurses had things under control — more or less.

"Welcome to the waiting game!" they told Matthew. "Take a number, any number, multiply by five. Divide by three, add a cup of tea, and what have you got?"

"I don't know," Matthew said.

"Neither do we!" the nurses all cried. "Sit down and wait. We'll call you when your number comes through, if it ever does."

"These two can't wait," said the ambulance guy. "They need an operation."

The waiting room was suddenly silent. Everyone turned to look. The midnight nurses stared at Matthew with big round eyes. "Operation?" they whispered. "Operation!" they shrieked, then they threw all their number cards into the air and started a frenzied conga line all around the waiting room.

Matthew and the injured squirrel were wheeled away into separate rooms. Matthew tried to lie flat and still, but the lights were bright and the air had a chill that made him shiver. It was very quiet. The students and doctors and TV crews who were sitting in the gallery were talking in whispers. Even the nurses were somewhat subdued. They shushed each other repeatedly, and hardly giggled at all. Suddenly the door swung open and the midnight surgeon appeared.

"What have we got?" he asked.

Matthew rolled up his pajama leg to let the surgeon see. The gallery gasped. The nurses shrieked. Everyone stared at Matthew's knee.

The surgeon frowned and shook his head. "It'll have to come off," he said.

The midnight surgeon held out his hand. "Scalpel, please."

"Scalpel! Scalpel!" the nurses all cried, as they ran around looking for one.

"Never mind," said the surgeon. "I'll just pull it off by hand. Stand back. Don't talk. Don't even breathe. On my count now, one . . . two . . . three!"

He reached over to Matthew's knee and pulled off the Band-Aid. The gallery began to cheer, but the surgeon held up his hand for silence.

"It's not over yet," he told them. "The most difficult part is still to come. How are you holding out there, son?"

"It didn't really hurt at all," Matthew told him.

"Brave lad! Quickly, Nurse! Bring me a transplant."

A midnight nurse soon arrived and in no time at all the midnight surgeon had a fresh new Band-Aid on Matthew's knee.

The midnight nurses wheeled Matthew into the recovery room. The injured squirrel was already there. His eyes were wide open and he looked much better.

"I'm Danny," he said with a shy little smile. "Thanks for taking care of me."

Suddenly the door burst open and a whole lot of squirrels ran in.

"You saved my brother!"

"My son!"

"My uncle!"

"I think he's my cousin."

Danny's family shook Matthew's hand and patted his back.

"We're the Flying Flingallees!" the father announced as the family struck a pose. "We've decided to put on a show to thank everyone in the hospital here. Only trouble is, Danny Boy is still recovering and we need him in the act."

"Could you take my place?" Danny asked Matthew. "I've seen you practice. You're really good."

So Matthew joined the Flying Flingallees and helped them do all their tricks. They did loop-the-loops on the flying trapeze, the Tightrope of Terror, the Amazing Acrobat Pyramid of Peril, and various other stupendous routines. The midnight nurses got into it too. They played their kazoos in a circusy way, while they danced and swayed and wiggled their bums wearing bedpans on their heads.

When it was time for the final trick, Danny announced loud and clear, "And now for the most magnificent, magical circus trick of all. The Flying Flingallees' never-performed-before, Fantastic Bombastic Human Cannon Ball!"

"Are you sure this will work?" Matthew asked, as they lowered him in.

"Not really," the father squirrel said. "But you're the only human we've got, so it's best if you think so." He loaded the cannon with dynamite, then added some more, just to make sure it was right. He lit the fuse and started the countdown. "Five . . . four . . . three . . . two . . . one . . ."

KAAABOOOOOM!!!

It was a huge and mighty blast, a real moonshot. It blew Matthew right through the open window.

The Flying Flingallees grabbed Matthew's boots as he flew up into the sky. "Goodbye!" they cried to the crowd down below. "We hope you enjoyed the show."

"What about Danny?" Matthew asked, as they arced through the night like a shooting star.

"The ambulance guys will bring him back to your garage," said the squirrels. "We're coming down again. That looks like your house ahead."

"I hope I left my window up," Matthew said nervously.

Luckily, he had done just that and they all landed together on the bed. "That sure was fun," Matthew laughed.

Everyone agreed. Danny's father drew the Flingallee crest on Matthew's Band-Aid. "Come be in our circus whenever you can. Just climb a tree and join our clan." Then one by one the Flying Flingallees waved goodbye and jumped out the window.

Matthew waved back, then he got into bed. He closed his eyes and soon he was fast asleep.

When Matthew woke up the following day, he checked his Band-Aid right away to see if it was still stuck on OK. It was. Then he ran into his mother's room to find out if she was awake. She wasn't, but she opened one eye when Matthew arrived.

"Matthew Holmes, it's six a.m. Stop jumping on my bed!" she said.

"Open up the garage door, Mom! We have to let Danny go!"

"Danny who?" his mother asked, as she closed her eye again.

"You know, the squirrel, the one that got hurt. Come on, he's waiting for us."

It took a bit of time to do, but Matthew finally got his mother down to the garage.

"Now, don't get your hopes up," she said as she lifted the heavy door. "That squirrel was pretty sick last night. He may be worse today."

She was wrong about that. As they approached the cardboard box the squirrel jumped up and dashed away out through the door.

"I can't believe it!" Matthew's mother said. "He's as good as new!"

"Of course he is. He had an operation, Mom. I went with him to Emergency and had one too," Matthew explained. His mother didn't quite understand, so he told her about the Flying Flingallees and the hospital circus show.

"That's the Flying Flingallee crest," he said, and pointed to his Band-Aid. "I'm part of their act now, you can be too, that is if you fit in the cannon."